For Lily and Whit, and for Rick, who always believed — M.C.

For my mother, who taught me to see with kindness — C.L.

Dial Books for Young Readers
Penguin Young Readers Group
An imprint of Penguin Random House LLC
375 Hudson Street, New York, NY 10014

Text copyright © 2018 Marcy Campbell. Illustration copyright © 2018 Corinna Luyken.

Printed in China • ISBN 9780735230378
10 9 8 7 6 5 4 3 2 1

Design by Lily Malcom
Text set in Filosofia

The art for this book was created using black ink,
colored pencils, and watercolor.

With gratitude to Steven Malk,
Namrata Tripathi, and Lily Malcom,
whose vision made this book possible.

Adrian Simcox Does NOT Have a Horse

written by Marcy Campbell   illustrated by Corinna Luyken

Dial Books for Young Readers

Adrian Simcox sits all by himself,
probably daydreaming again.

And Adrian Simcox tells anyone who will
listen that he has a horse.

Some kids believe him. But I don't.

He lives in town like me, and I know you can't have a horse in town.

"Where would he put it?" I asked Jamie at recess. Jamie said Adrian lives with his grandpa, and their house is very small, and there's hardly any yard.

She said, "The horse goes to the country sometimes, that's what Adrian said."

"Ha!" Jamie will believe anything.

I told my mom about Adrian's horse and how he definitely does not have one.

"Hmmm," she said. "And how would you know, Ms. Smarty-Pants?"

"Because I know! Adrian Simcox does NOT have a horse!" Adrian Simcox gets the free lunch at school. His shoes have holes. Kelsey told me her cousin has a horse, and it's super expensive. He can't take care of a horse.

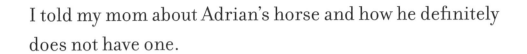

Adrian Simcox can't even take care of his own desk.

Our teacher always says, "We must try to be understanding. We have to be patient."

But I was tired of being patient with Adrian Simcox and tired of trying to understand why he kept telling everybody he had a horse when HE DID NOT!

The next day by the swings he was telling a bunch of little kids about his "beautiful horse with its white coat and golden mane," saying she had "the biggest, brownest eyes of any horse, anywhere."

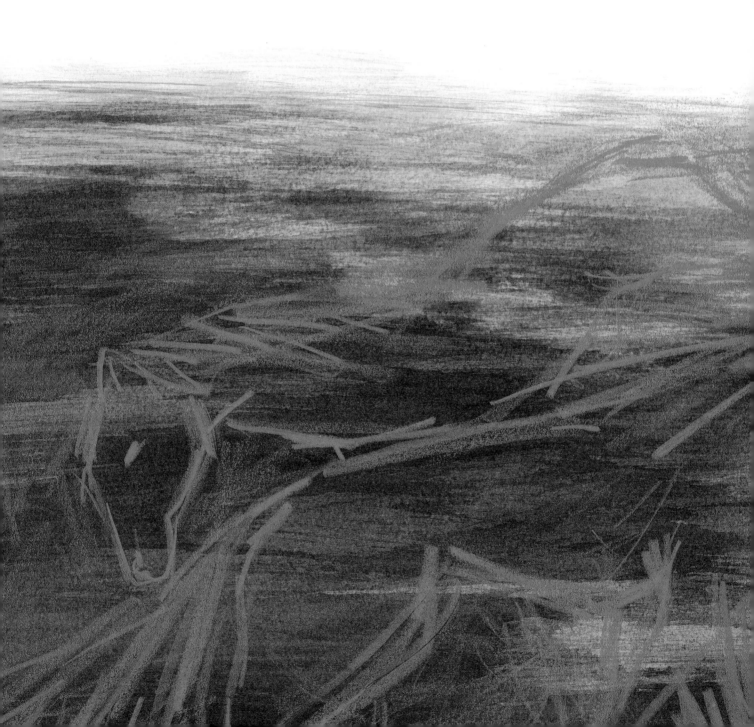

So I yelled from the monkey bars,
"He's lying! Adrian Simcox does NOT have a horse!"

Even though I was upside down,
I could see that made Adrian Simcox really sad.

That night I told my mom how Adrian was lying about his horse again, and she said, "Chloe, it's time to take Chompers for his walk."

A little dog is a perfectly normal pet to have in town.

Mom walked even faster than usual, so I had to run with Chompers to keep up. But when she got to the corner where we always turn left, she turned right.

"Why are we going over here?" I asked. Chompers loved it, but I didn't.

All the houses looked like they might fall down, and even though it wasn't trash day, it looked like it was.

But Mom kept walking. When someone said "Evening," she said "Evening" right back.

And then I saw him, Adrian Simcox, at a little house down the street.

I stopped walking. Chompers kept pulling.
"That's Adrian Simcox," I said.
"Yes, I know. I met his grandpa at the back-to-school picnic. Now, come on," said Mom.

It was the tiniest house I ever saw. It was like half of our house.

Mom started talking to Adrian's grandpa, and Adrian said,
"I like your dog."

Chompers pulled the leash from my hand and went
over and licked Adrian Simcox, right on the face!
I could see the backyard. It was no place for
a horse, that's for sure.

I could feel some words coming up in my throat and tangling in there, like when I swallowed something and it went down the wrong pipe.

You. Do. Not. Have. A. Horse.

But I didn't say it because of how Adrian was looking and how it reminded me of when I told those little kids he was lying.

Adrian Simcox tossed a ball to me.
I caught it. I tossed it back to him.

It was kind of cool to see Adrian Simcox smile.

So I asked him, "Is your horse at a farm?"

And Adrian started talking about his horse "with a white coat and
golden mane and the biggest, brownest eyes of any horse, anywhere. . . ."

And then I thought Adrian Simcox had just about the best imagination of any kid in our whole school.

I also thought, he had the most beautiful horse of anyone, anywhere.